OF
SERPENT
DREAMS

OF SERPENT DREAMS

J. ZACHARIAS

Ragged Bears

First published in 2022 by Ragged Bears Ltd

Sherborne, DT9 3PH

www.ragged-bears.co.uk

ISBN: 9781857144918

1 2 3 4 5 6 7 8 9 10

A CIP catalogue record for this book is available
from the British Library

Printed and bound in Great Britain
by Clays Ltd, Elcograf S.p.A.

*Dedicated to the strong and beautiful ladies in my life:
my mother, Matilda D'Silva, my sisters, Irene Hilda
and Marilyn Ragi and my precious nieces,
Elizabeth Antonia and Hannah Maria.*

*For my grandmothers who I never had the privilege of
being with but I know would love their spirits present in
Anitha's life: Reginal D'Silva and Penial Joosa.*

*For Neng and Kim: Thank you for being a constant
support for the family in more ways than one.*

*For my feline friends: Dexter, Blackie, Mr Tiggs and all
the village cats that have graced my world. Thank you
for the gift of animal magnetism.*

*To the City of York, the River Ouse and the Greenway for
being constant wells of inspiration that sustain my creative
spirit - thank you a thousand times and more . . .*

*For all my beloved readers who choose to journey
with Anitha on her inner and outer travels,
she's grateful for the companionship.*

*Finally, to that beautiful, shining adder I encountered
on the moors in September 2019, thank you for the
spellbinding moment when nothing mattered but
you, me and infinity . . .*

PROLOGUE

She walked along the trail and cut across the farmland with its tidy, sprayed fields. The trail yielded to another dirt path that led her to the forest; the woods, old as time itself. Wild flowers carpeted the ground beneath her feet. Thirstily, she sucked in the clean, fresh air.

Walking on ahead, she paused abruptly to where a coven of ancient yews stood, all gnarled, bent and twisted. Yards away, the murmur of a rivulet urged her on. A trill of birds echoed amidst the shrouding trees.

Her knees dropped to the soft, damp soil. Fingers reached out to the lure of the cool, clear running water.

Suddenly...

Like bullet shots, pain shot across her limbs. Drone-like buzzing penetrated her ears. Sun rays stung red-hot. Cold shivers weaved through her bones. Blinking, she rose with a groan. A chill lent an empty feeling inside her. The soles of her bare feet scraped against the burning tarmac of a long, eternal street flanked either side with tall, concrete buildings. A few dull-eyed people walked past, glued to their gadgets.

The landscape before her tear-stung eyes was bereft of trees, grass, water, flowers…no birdsong cheered the air. All was gravely still and silent except for the whirr of machine-like white noise.

Terrified, she clutched her throat which was sandy-dry and swiftly closing in on her breath. She choked, gasped…

PART 1

PART 1

CHAPTER ONE

Anitha rushed down the stairs to the delicious scent of lemon-drizzled buckwheat pancakes. On the window sill of the dining room, she stopped to water her miniature bamboo plant. It was a gift from Grandma.

"You're late," chided Durga as she flipped two pancakes onto a plate and topped them with maple syrup. Her daughter did not reply.

While showering, Anitha had decided to refrain from sharing last night's dream with her mother. She sensed her mother was still raw, wounded and slowly healing from her meltdown last year. Although accustomed to strange and vivid dreams, Anitha was disturbed by this particular dream. No. Nightmare.

Hungry, she tucked into her breakfast while sipping hot lemon verbena tea. Minutes later, she was good to go. Thanks to her dear grandpa, her father's father who had passed away last year in December, Anitha was now able to afford to attend the prestigious St Hilda's College for Girls. It was situated a few villages away on a hill surrounded by acres of lush, green land. A college-owned bus picked up girls from the various points and dropped them off before nine in the morning. Classes commenced at nine and ended at four in the afternoon, after which the bus would return the girls home. It was Grandpa's inheritance that enabled Anitha to afford the luxury of this education and for that she would be forever grateful. She had worked hard and earned her place in the college and Grandpa would be proud of her.

Durga started the dishwasher. "Our new neighbours have been here a week. I've seen a young girl your age. We must say hello…this evening?"

"Sure," Anitha mumbled as she kissed her mother goodbye.

Durga observed her daughter's smart uniform – a pale, long-sleeved, purple blouse with a pleated black skirt that fell just above her knees, black stockings and a black, tailored coat. "Goodness! Don't you look all grown-up and serious!"

"Please…I've always been grown-up and serious!"

* * *

Outside, the October winds picked up speed. The front garden, pathway and driveway were littered with leaves of deep red and golden yellow. Through the hedges, a sparrow chirped. Anitha threw a handful of seeds. Immediately, the bird came into view along with a robin and they began pecking. Soon, two blackbirds joined the feast. A door slammed. Anitha looked up to see a huge van with two men lifting furniture. A girl in a wheelchair with a floral printed blanket over her knees waved to her. Anitha walked over.

"Hello," the girl beamed.

"Hello," Anitha smiled. "Welcome to the village."

"Thanks. I'm Alhena. Alhena Regina. Call me Ally for short."

"I'm Anitha."

"Meet Jag."

"Jag?"

"Jag." Alhena Regina tapped the metallic arm of her wheelchair. "My other half. The Jaguar of all wheelchairs."

"Hello, Jag." Jag was certainly impressive – huge, super-shiny and kitted with multi-functional buttons. Clearly, Jag was top of the range. Instinctively, Anitha touched Jag. The metal felt cold and smooth and clean like solid water. All at once, shadows swirled like ribbons around Anitha, interlocking Jag with her hand. Almost immediately, Anitha removed her hand. "Sorry," she apologised, embarrassed. "I didn't mean to touch you…I mean Jag. That was rude of me."

Alhena Regina was now staring into Anitha's eyes. "That's okay."

"Which college do you attend?" Anitha tried to ease the awkwardness.

"I'm home-schooled."

"Oh."

"Your eyes…" Alhena Regina said, still staring.

"Excuse me?"

"They seem to be changing colour…"

Anitha stepped back.

Alhena Regina blinked. Gold flecks slid across her neighbour's small, dark eyes. She shook her head. "It must be the sun in your eyes," she dismissed somewhat unconvincingly.

"Well, I have a bus to catch! See you around!"

The last person she wanted to see at the front street bus-stop was Solomon, riding his bicycle in all his six-foot plus gorgeousness. His hair, ruffled and bathed in autumnal hues gleamed in the morning rays.

How annoying!

He stopped in front of Anitha. Girls peeled their eyes away from their smartphones to objectify the supreme icon of male specimen leaning against his beat-up bike. Boys pretended not to notice.

Ugh.

Anitha pulled her woollen, blue scarf closer to her chin. Her heart beat extra fast.

"Hey," Solomon started.

Anitha turned her head away. She heard a collective gasp from the lurking female tribe. Where was the bus?

"You're off to St Hilda's, I hear. Posh girl," he teased, grinning that lopsided grin of his that set her heart afire many moons ago. "We should meet up," Solomon persisted.

"Seriously, Sol? For someone who has not said a word since December, you sure have a lot to say," Anitha blurted. She felt the army of girls retreat. They can have him, she swore to herself.

"I needed time."

"Take more."

"We need to talk," Solomon sounded irritated.

The nerve. "Go away!"

"I know you," Solomon lowered his voice and edged closer.

"Whatever."

Solomon's green eyes bored into her. "I know who you are," he whispered.

Anitha froze. "Wh...what? How?" she hissed.

"It takes one to know one." With that Solomon hopped on his bike and rode off, disappearing around the corner.

CHAPTER TWO

It was the weekend and Anitha was scribbling notes for her recent project: the demonisation of female archetypes in ancient myths – when her mother called out to her. She ignored the call.

Durga appeared at the bedroom doorway. "Right. I have prepared some soup for the new neighbours and you're coming with me to officially welcome them."

"Now?"

"Now."

"Busy." In actuality, Anitha was still self-conscious from the encounter with Ally last Monday.

"I'm not asking."

A tall, bespectacled man in his fifties with grey hair answered the door.

"Good afternoon, we live next door. I'm Durga and this is my daughter, Anitha. I've made some bean and vegetable soup for the family to welcome you to the village."

Genuinely pleased, the man exclaimed, "Why thank you! Thank you! I'm Amos, pleased to make your acquaintance. Come in, come in. It's rather chilly. I'll prepare some coffee."

"Er," Durga hesitated. She was tempted to go in for a chat but she did promise Anitha only five minutes of introduction. "It is very sweet of you but I must decline your offer. My daughter has homework and er…"

"I understand. Well, another time then. Coffee and cake. I insist." Amos studied Anitha quietly. "My niece told me she had already met you in the early week."

"Niece?" For a split second, Anitha spied YinYang, the black and white stray cat slink past her legs. He turned, met her eyes and disappeared under the bushes.

"Yes, Alhena is my niece. I'm her uncle."

Just then, a pale gold Mercedes entered the driveway and parked beside a black Jaguar. Another man in his fifties with sleek, silver hair and dressed in a finely cut suit, stepped out swinging a leather briefcase.

"And that is Levi, my partner," Amos introduced.

Durga and Anitha shook hands and exchanged pleasantries with Levi. Durga turned to Amos, "Thank you, Amos for the invite. I will certainly take you up on your offer and please, if you need anything at all, I'll be glad to help."

"Very kind of you. Likewise. Likewise."

"Enjoy the soup."

"We most certainly will."

CHAPTER THREE

It was her time of the month. That explained her bloating, mood swings and more than the usual intense dreams. Grandma had told her that dreams would be lucid during her period.

Grandma. Amama. Her mother's mother in Kerala. It had been more than a year since her first visit there. What a year it had been. A year of revelations that had entirely turned her once little world upside down, inside out.

Hastily, Anitha slipped on her college uniform.

"You're late again."

"Mmm…"

"Is there something you want to tell me or talk to me about?" Durga put the kettle on.

Anitha spread some almond butter on to a quinoa rice cake and bit into it. "Nah. It's just the time of the month."

Durga steeped a rooibos teabag into her mug of hot water. "Oh, right. Then this evening, don't forget to…"

Anitha interrupted, "I know, I know. The Bath." She sipped her lemon infused hot water.

Leaning against the counter top, Durga crossed her arms and remarked, "You really are on top of this, aren't you? It's only been about a year and already you are comfortable about your different skins. Your grandma will be really proud of you."

SKINS.

Anitha pondered on the word. Human skin. Serpentine skin. Skins from two separate realms. Skins that opened doors of infinite possibilities.

The Bath was essential, of utmost necessity, Grandma had warned her. Her naga skin would need to manifest and express itself before shedding in the bath. Like the shedding of her human blood, her naga side needed to shed for the sake of survival and renewal. If she ignored this process, her blood would be slowly poisoned.

"It's a commitment, Ma, and I plan to be committed to myself."

"Of course sweetheart. Now finish up. I've a long

day at the nursery so I'll be late. I'll leave dinner in the fridge."

"Okay."

"Oh, and don't forget to top up the bird feeder when you get back and sort the recycling for tomorrow."

Anitha kissed her mum. "Okay."

Durga put the kettle on for a second cup of tea. "Oh, by the way, this project of yours, on female archetypes...how is that going? Did you pick any archetype in particular?"

Buttoning up her coat, Anitha waited a few seconds before replying, "Medusa, of course."

There were six of them in the bus on its way to St Hilda's. Anitha stared out of the window as the bus moved on. Falling leaves drifted and danced in the chilly air before softly landing on the ground. Leaves of green, yellow and pale reds soaked in hints of gold washed the landscape with its final burst of splendour.

Feeling sleepy, Anitha decided to cat nap before the bus arrived at the college. There were still a few more stops to go. She tried to push away the nightmare from last night. Yawning, she inhaled and exhaled deeply until she felt her limbs lose their tension. Her chest rose and fell steadily.

Suddenly, the bus stopped. Anitha's eyes flew open. As she looked around, she gasped. The five other girls in the bus were sat still, their eyes, vacant and gazing into computer screens attached to the seats in front of them. Their skins were pale and ashen. All were dressed in black and white. Outside the bus window, Anitha saw spinning, insect-like gadgets shrouding daylight with their mechanical presence. Instead of the chatter of birds there was the whirr of drones. However, it was the absence of trees and grass and wildlife that shook her to her bones. In their place was what appeared in her eyes to be an endless horizon of black tarmac and buildings packed together resembling industrial warehouses or prisons.

Quickly, Anitha shut her eyes tightly. Her heart hammered. Her skin felt hot and cold, smooth and scaly all at the same time. Her legs tingled in a wobbly manner. No, no, Anitha prayed silently, not now, not now, please. In the evening, The Bath, I promise, please. Think of Grandma, she urged herself, think of Grandma, Grandma…Grandma's face flashed briefly in her mind, her sweet, small, dark face and silver hair in a high bun. That strong, assuring smile and golden-brown eyes that centred Anitha in this state of panic.

A hush fell.

The bus stopped. Anitha opened her eyes. Relieved to return to normal vision, she breathed evenly. Two girls got on the bus. One, she recognised, the Japanese girl who lived in a student accommodation flat, but the other she did not. Towering at six-foot, this girl was porcelain-white with pale blonde hair that reached her broad shoulders and eyes that were an electric blue. She scanned the bus and her piercing gaze landed on Anitha. There were plenty of seats available but she chose to sit herself beside Anitha.

"Hi," she said.

"Hi," Anitha acknowledged. The girl reminded her of some creature that had just emerged from a Grimm's fairy tale.

Crossing her ankles, the girl continued, "Who are you?" Her eyes were intent on Anitha.

Anitha detected a northern European accent. "Who are you?"

The girl broke into a smile. "Mathilda."

"Anitha."

"First year?"

"Yes. You?"

"Second."

"I've not seen you in the bus before."

"Oh, I'm a boarder. I stay at the college but this weekend I stayed with my guardian. I needed the privacy."

"I've seen the dormitories. They are beautiful."

"Well they should be! It's expensive to board – but that's okay. What subjects do you study?"

"Woman's Studies, Mathematics and Physics. You?"

"Interesting combination. Me? Botany, Social Sciences and Art." Mathilda uncrossed her ankles and seemed to be thinking. "I see your eyes," she whispered, ever so softly.

Anitha stiffened.

"I see your eyes and I can share with you…"

Unwilling to engage in the conversation, Anitha looked out of the window.

"Don't worry. I will not tell a soul."

Anitha sealed her lips shut.

"It is not often that I see what I see in your eyes."

Anitha had had enough. "Could you please sit elsewhere? I like my space."

"What do you know about St Hilda's?"

"Excuse me?"

"What do you know about St. Hilda's? The history."

Sighing, Anitha answered. There was something about Mathilda that drew her. "St. Hilda's was named after the 7th century English saint and abbess; the one from Whitby."

"That is untrue. That is a lie they keep telling the students' parents and I am so tired of it." Mathilda grumbled.

Intrigued, Anitha asked, "I don't understand."

"I will tell you but you must not interrupt."

"Okay."

Staring into space, Mathilda began, "Centuries ago, there was a peasant woman, Flora who lived in the mountains of the Black Forest in Germany. Some say she was a witch, a witch who worshipped the ancient Goddess Holda."

Anitha bit her lip. Holda. Hilda. Hmmm…

"As a child, Flora was abused badly by her parents. One morning, as the story goes, she fell into a well. Was it attempted murder or was it suicide? Either way, she encountered the Goddess Holda in the well."

The Well. Anitha held her breath as she remembered her own experience last year.

"Flora was made to complete chores which she did dutifully simply because she was an obedient child. Besides, Holda did not take kindly to lazy beings. It was an offence punishable by death or a life of curse. One day, the Goddess called Flora to her and expressed her satisfaction with Flora's industrious nature and rewarded her with freedom. Flora was free to leave The Well but not before the Goddess bestowed her with gold and wealth beyond belief.

Flora grew up and put her good fortune to benevolent use. The poor and sick thrived under her care. Due to her contact with the Goddess herself, she gained access to the knowledge and power of magick."

The bus stopped and two more girls got on. There were ten minutes to go before the bus arrived at the college. Eager for the story to continue, Anitha said, "Go on."

A sadness washed across Mathilda's face as she narrated the next part of the strange tale. "Flora never forgot her benefactor and worshipped the Goddess Holda secretly, making shrines in woods, forests, caves...but a witch hunt forced her to flee...with her firstborn, a baby boy."

"How horrible."

"Yes. She moved through various towns and villages. Soon, she settled for a common life as a wife and mother to avert suspicions. She had several sons and daughters and lived the life of a normal person. Whatever normal is."

"How is this linked to St. Hilda's?" Anitha asked.

"Flora's descendants thrived and migrated all over the world. Some settled here in England and opened a private college for girls, The Holda College for Girls."

Closing her eyes, Anitha said, "Now I see."

"With time, the name was anglicised, Christianised to St Hilda's after the nun from Whitby. It was more acceptable."

The bus finally turned into a long, winding private road. Acres of rural land welcomed the students.

Horses and sheep grazed peacefully. Woodland stretched for miles. Uphill the bus went and soon the upward sweep of the stony, dark, gothic presence of the cathedral design of St Hilda's, with its flying buttresses and menacing gargoyles, loomed magnificently in a haunting embrace heavenwards.

Spellbound by the narration, Anitha asked, "How did you come to know of this?"

A moment of quiet passed before Mathilda answered, "I am a descendant of Flora."

CHAPTER FOUR

Her skins stirred as her limbs eased in the warm, sandalwood infused bathwater. Pinprick sensations caused her to flinch. The pain was distressing.

Looking at her outstretched arms, Anitha observed the intermingling of her human epidermis layer with the pushing and emerging of luminous, glassy serpentine scales. It had been a year and the awesome sight still took her breath away. However, she prayed that the pain would lessen with time.

She forced her mind to think other thoughts – the new girl next door, Alhena Regina, and her uncle Amos...what had happened to her parents? And Jag, her metallic soulmate with a life of its own... that unnerved Anitha; then there was Mathilda, the strange German girl with an intriguing past. She must remember to invite Mathilda over for a stay. Finally, Solomon – what did he mean by "It takes one to know one"? Was he like her? If so, that would explain why he remembered her changing from last year when everyone else had no memory of it. And the recent nightmares – the dystopian scenes – they terrified her. Were they prophetic or simply her imagination let loose?

Amama. Grandma. "All you have to do is think of me and I'll be there," Amama had assured her. So Anitha did. Closing her eyes, she whispered, "Amama, Amama, Amama…". The warm steam rose with the scent of sandalwood before swirling in delicate circles.

"You called?"

Dreamily, Anitha opened her sleepy eyes. Veiled beneath the bathwater, her grandmother's impassive face emerged from among the floating human and serpentine skins. "Amama…"

"Yes, dear." The voice was distant with a slight echo.

"They haunt me…" a drowsiness was taking over Anitha.

"What haunts you, baby girl?"

"Dreams…no, nightmares…they scare me. I can't explain them. Help me, Amama…"

"Listen, sweetheart."

Although in deep sleep, Anitha's mind was awake and she heard her grandma loud and clear. It was weird.

"Water has memory," her grandmother continued, "it absorbs information. It records everything and stores all data accurately for all time. It is also a portal of transmission. I need you to retrieve your dreams so I can see what haunts you."

"Uh, okay," Anitha mumbled.

"Good. Now, breathe in and focus."

Anitha obeyed. For a while no one spoke and nothing happened. Her mind was blank but she was aware of her human skin shedding. Her emotions swung from pain to euphoria. Suddenly, she felt a fresh, powerful pulse whoosh through her entire body. The steaming air hissed, crackled and sparked. The nightmares of the recent past gushed forth in her mind. The bathwater bubbled with heat and cold. Scenes of a dystopian nature unfolded in ripples. Sterile, greyish-white landscapes took on a more intensified bleakness. Sounds of machines deafened her ears. Yeasty-skinned humans dragged their feet in dull paces. The naga within Anitha magnified each sensory assault. She feared she would implode.

"Return," her grandmother commanded.

For a few brief moments, Anitha juddered before returning to her current senses. Her grandmother waited patiently till she settled into regular breathing. "I see," she said quietly, her face undulating gently with the movement of the bathwater.

"What do you see, Amama?" Anitha asked in sheer exhaustion.

"The Apocalypse."

"The what?"

"The Apocalypse, the end of this earth we were gifted with since the beginning of time."

"I don't understand."

"You were given access to these dreams for a reason. It's your calling. Your destiny."

"But..." Anitha was now completely adorned in her scales. She gazed admiringly at herself as the waters reflected the diamond-hued flickers of her new skin. "What should I do?"

"You will know what to do when the time arrives."

"But for now, Amama?"

"Wait."

"Wait," Anitha repeated, absently, still mesmerised by her other worldly beauteous form.

CHAPTER FIVE

Smugly, Kamini Smith smiled as she signed the last of the documents. Leaning back on her office chair, she tapped her gold pen on the large, polished mahogany table.

Finally. Her vision, her dream was coming to fruition. This was the icing on the cake. All other property development projects could not hold a candle to this one. She, Kamini Smith was the prime mover and shaker of this multi-billion-pound project.

She could smell the money. Mmm...

Her mobile buzzed. "Yes, yes...of course, darling... I'm all packed. What about the children? Good, good...make sure Liam has his teddy...he won't be able to sleep without him and remind Maia to pack her pink bathing suit. The one with the flamingo. I'll be there in an hour. Just leaving. We'll grab something on the way...sure...sure...see you..."

While whistling a tune, Kamini Smith sorted a few papers into her briefcase. She was certainly looking forward to the weekend on the Greek islands with the family on a friend's yacht – lounging in the sun, free flow of champagne, snacking on caviar… There was a knock on the door.

"Come in!" Kamini checked her watch. A bespectacled, young man in his late twenties walked in. "Yes? What is it?"

"Er. We had an appointment?" He sounded nervous.

"Now?" Kamini frowned.

"Er…yes." He stood by the door, unsure of stepping further in.

Irritated, Kamini gestured to him to sit down. "What is this regarding? You're John, right?"

"Yes, from the project coordination department."

"Right, sit."

John sat on the edge of the seat facing her. Her sharp nose and high cheekbones gave her a severe expression.

"Well? What is this regarding?" Kamini was almost done sorting her papers.

John hesitated a few seconds, cleared his throat and began to explain that on behalf of his department, he would like to request a raise.

"Bring it up at the next company meeting. We'll have a discussion about it." Kamini checked her watch again. If she left in the next few minutes, she could beat traffic.

"Er. We did bring it up a few months ago."

"Bring it up again. I am sorry, John. I have to make a move. I promise, before Christmas, we'll come up with something."

John watched her smile, a pretend smile. For three years, he and his department had been asking for a raise but to no avail. They were beginning to get restless. Lies and procrastination. He was aware that Kamini was on her way to the Greek islands. She could afford it. Not him and certainly not those in his department. His wife had just been made redundant and last year his firstborn was diagnosed with autism. He could do with the raise. The medical bills were beginning to take a toll on both his wife and himself. His wife was crying everyday and he had taken to secretly drinking. He had mentioned his son's condition in the previous meeting thinking he could appeal to Kamini's maternal side. She simply smiled that fake smile with the tilt of her head and made an empty promise that she would look into it as soon as possible.

It wasn't just about him. His team members usually worked late hours and for the past five years had not received a single raise nor a Christmas bonus. They too had their own personal challenges. Karen had just lost her father to a stroke and now cared for her mother who suffered with dementia. A raise could help with the bills. May, a single mother with two sons under the age of five, was just making ends meet. And after the sudden death of his brother two years ago, Sam had promised to support his brother's family till his sister-in-law, Tina was back on her feet, but he had discovered recently that she was addicted to prescription drugs and barely coping.

Despite personal challenges, each one of his department peers turned up for work dutifully. Surely, they deserved to be heard and rewarded.

"John?"

John snapped from his thoughts. Kamini had said something. Probably, more lies. "Yes?"

"I promise. Schedule another meeting a couple of weeks before Christmas. Don't worry about it. We'll see if we can come to some sort of arrangement." She locked her briefcase and slipped on her heels. "Close the door behind you. Thanks." Again, that fake smile and words as slick as oil.

Defeated, John got up and left.

CHAPTER SIX

Perched on the outside window sill, YinYang yawned as he peered through the bay window, watching Anitha busy on her computer. Anitha felt his feline green eyes boring into her, but she knew her mother would not allow the stray indoors.

"God knows where he's been and what he's been up to...he's not welcome in my house!" Durga had put her foot down.

It was the Bank Holiday weekend and Anitha had already spent hours on her Medusa project. Piles of research materials cluttered the dining room table. She shook her head at the cat and returned to review the first few pages of her work on the computer.

...It did not matter whether Medusa

consented to her relationship with Poseidon. In the eyes of patriarchy, she was and is condemned as a figure of fear and repulsion. Prior to her assassination by Perseus who was and is hailed as a hero, Medusa was a beautiful, wise and powerful feminine force who gained access to magic and communed with the gods. According to some theories, she was deft in the art of healing and was blessed with the gift of prophecy.

This clearly offended and terrified the elite and mostly male counterparts of her time and they deemed it worthy to eliminate such a female force who was clearly out of line in their eyes.

"Off with her head" was patriarchy's solution to keeping women in their place. To this day, the movie industry has glorified this homicide, a lesson, perhaps to modern women?

YinYang scratched his claws on the window pane. Biting her lip, Anitha sighed and opened the window. "Only for a while. Mum's having a nap." YinYang leapt, landing on her cluttered table. Picking him up gently, Anitha stroked his soft fur. She was missing Ebony, so cruelly taken away from her last year during the assault on Halloween night. As for Solomon, she could only imagine his loss. After all, Ebony was his cat. They never did talk about that night – she and Solomon.

The doorbell rang. YinYang slipped from Anitha's embrace and padded out of the door as soon she opened it.

It was Alhena Regina. "Hey."

Anitha grinned to see YinYang rub himself against Jag's wheels. "Hey."

"He's too cute."

"Yeah. Not mine. Mum doesn't let him in the house. He's a stray."

"Your secret's safe with me."

Arching his back sleekly, YinYang stretched upwards and pawed at Alhena's knee blanket before helping himself to her lap.

"Uh oh…he owns you now," Anitha warned teasingly.

Alhena giggled. "My tutor's just left. It's a beautiful, sunny day. I was wondering if you'd like to join me on the Greenway. Amos says as long as I come back way before dark…I'd love to see the village countryside."

Anitha thought for a moment. She would leave a note for mum. Alhena was right. The day was bright and dry. Her project could wait till evening.

The October breeze was cold and fresh but the sun with its golden, warm kisses lifted the spirits.

Alhena reduced Jag's speed so she could let Anitha walk beside her at a leisurely pace. A squirrel dashed out in front of them. "Thanks for coming out with me."

"Oh please. I'm glad to be away from the computer."

The girls paused to say hello to a dogwalker and pat his three dogs. "So, what do you study?" Anitha asked.

"Art History, Literature and Media Marketing. Have you ever heard of Ivan Bilibin?"

Anitha said no.

"He was a Russian artist. He painted the most beautiful paintings in the world. Fairy-tale paintings. One day, I hope to paint like him."

"You paint?"

"Yes. It keeps me…well…it keeps me real…I feel my best when I am painting."

"I would love to see some of your artwork, if that's okay…and the Russian artist you mentioned…"

"Sure. I would like that." Alhena put a brake on Jag. "This countryside is truly awesome," she stared into the space before her.

Anitha scanned the expansive, autumnal landscape of farmland and woods. "Yes. It is. There is an ancient wood further along, if you are interested but Jag… um…"

"Jag's pretty competent on most diverse terrains."

"The ground will be wet – soft and leafy," Anitha added, hesitantly.

"I'm sure Jag will handle it. He's built like a superhero."

"I'm impressed," admitted Anitha, drawing a smile.

"With money, almost anything is possible…" Alhena whispered, quite sadly.

Leading the way, Anitha turned down a quiet track. Jag followed.

"You must be wondering what happened to me," Alhena started.

Avoiding the brambles, Anitha jumped to a clearer space. "I'll tell my story then you tell yours."

Taken aback by Anitha's bluntness, Alhena simply nodded.

"I lost my dad to a car crash when I was a baby. I lived. He didn't. My family feel it should have been me. He was a good man and well-loved. I suffered nightmares for years. I still do but not as frequently. So there." It seemed strange to Anitha to speak of the tragedy that had defined her entire life in a matter of fact way. "So, what about you?" The wood was almost in sight.

"My mum killed herself after I was born because she was grieving for her other baby."

Anitha stopped in her tracks. "Other baby?"

"Yeah. I was one of twins. She died in the womb

at eight months. I survived. Mum gave her a name. Regina."

Anitha's mouth fell open. "You've taken on her name as your second name?" It sounded creepy.

Feeling suddenly self-conscious, Alhena stumbled through the next few words defensively. "She was my other half. We literally shared the same womb. So why not."

"And your dad?"

"He left a year after mum poisoned herself. Amos, my dad's brother raised me. He's my sole guardian. Back in Israel, Amos was living in a three-storey mansion. When I was nine, I jumped from the rooftop."

"Good god, Ally."

"That's how I ended up with Jag. Amos went wild. He blamed himself. So, a few years back, Amos and I came here to live and leave all the horrid memories behind. He met Levi and we have been starting over ever since… but we never really get away, do we? It always haunts us – the pain, the grief…I have bad dreams all the time."

"You do?"

"I see shadows and monsters. They come after me and I am running…"

"And then?"

"I wake up, screaming and crying and Amos stays with me till I fall asleep again."

"I see."

"That is why I paint. It is the only time, I forget. When I paint, I am free…you understand, don't you, Anitha?"

Anitha felt as though someone had stuck a screwdriver into her heart and twisted it. "I do but… er…if you like, I could help you with your bad dreams…" Anitha blurted. She did not know why she said what she said.

"Help me?" That was not what Alhena Regina was expecting in response.

"My grandma – she says to always work with my dreams – not ignore them."

"Oh." Alhena Regina fell silent. What was she supposed to say?

The girls went ahead a few more yards before Anitha exclaimed, "The woods. We are here. This is ancient, sacred land. Being here helps me. It will help you too, Ally."

CHAPTER SEVEN

Fallen leaves left the trees almost bare. Sunshine poured through from the blue skies. The woody, slumbering air weaved through each tree, oak, yew, hawthorn, elder…

Alhena Regina breathed in. She felt the history of this place. Old, still and timeless…she heard the murmur of the river and directed Jag towards the crystal-clear flowing waters. Standing further down the winding river was Anitha, absorbed in her own world of contemplation. Around her towered tall, hunched and twisted yews. Banks of weeping willows bowed in elegant poses. A touch of sunlight cast a glow upon her shiny, black hair. The sight took Alhena's breath away. This was worthy of a painting. With her artistic eyes, she focussed and captured the sight in memory. There was something else that hit Alhena. It was as if Anitha belonged here, not elsewhere but here...with the river and the trees and the birds and the brambles and the streaking sunrays...

Suddenly, Anitha turned sharply. "Did you hear that?"

"Hear what?"

The air was still.

"That..."

A dim, wavering mist clouded the sunshine. A wind blew but it did not feel natural to Anitha. Instead, the wind felt conjured. From behind a grandfather oak, a form came into presence. Haltingly, Anitha stepped back. Her gut wrenched. It was a big, black, wild boar. She needed to save Alhena and herself. However, the boar did not advance. She's pregnant, Anitha noticed.

Immobilised, she eyed the boar. The boar eyed her back, its eyes dark and alive.

Once again, the air shattered with the clang of metallic sounds. Anitha covered her ears. The mist lifted.

"Anitha!"

Spinning around, she saw Solomon, his strong hand gripping her left wrist. Behind him was Alhena, white with shock and fear. Solomon bent and whispered in her ears, "Breathe..."

Anitha breathed.

"What happened to you, Ani?" Alhena's voice was

shaking. "You went still as a statue suddenly and, and your lips were moving but I couldn't hear anything…I was going to call Amos to come and get us but…but… he turned up…" she regarded Solomon shyly.

"I'm Solomon," he smiled.

With her eyes lowered, Alhena introduced herself.

"What are you doing here?" snapped Anitha, releasing from his grip.

"You're welcome. I was cycling on the Greenway and saw the two of you enter the woods."

"So, you thought you'd join us." Anitha crossed her arms.

"Maybe we should make our way back," Alhena suggested, timidly.

Solomon agreed, "Good idea."

CHAPTER EIGHT

"Before the end of this week, I'll sort a ramp out so your friend can come into our home for a drink and a meal." Guiltily, Durga closed the front door once they saw Alhena to her house. "It's a shame we can't invite her in now."

Rolling her eyes, Anitha bristled, "She's not my friend. She's a neighbour."

"Really, Anitha," chided Durga, "it would be nice for once to have people your age come over for anything."

"Please don't be desperate for me," remarked Anitha caustically, although she did consider Mathilda or as she called her, Tilly, for an invite. In the past few weeks, they had been getting to know each other really well. They sat next to each other in the bus and when free time permitted, they would spend lunch together, talking and sharing about almost everything. Anitha had yet to divulge to Tilly about her naga bloodline. However, Tilly was more than open about her own witch blood. Her milky, blue eyes gleamed supernaturally each time she gushed about spells and potions and forests and the unseen elementals that inhabit the natural world. Just like Anitha, Tilly was passionate about the earth but her all-consuming hatred against the human race did give Anitha the shivers.

"I'm still going to get a ramp built." Durga went to the kitchen and called out, "Would you care for a hot chocolate, Solomon?"

Awkwardly, Solomon stood at the threshold of the living room. Dreading his tall, sturdy, testosterone fuelled presence, Anitha interjected, "He's just leaving Ma!" She proceeded to open the front door.

"Yes! I'd like one, please!" Solomon answered for himself.

Glowering at his cheeky grin, Anitha flounced into the living room and threw herself on the sofa. "Really?"

Durga set three mugs of hot chocolate dusted with cinnamon and nutmeg on the front table before getting comfortable on her armchair. Seated opposite Anitha was Solomon, his intrusively long legs stretching out in front of her. As much as she resisted, she could not deny the feeling of being soothed whenever he was around. Only one other person beside Solomon was capable of that – Amama.

With probing green eyes, Solomon began, "What happened in the woods?"

It was best to get the experience off her chest. "...I...I had my back turned to Ally...watching, listening to the river and out of nowhere...this...this wind rose and a mist fell..."

"A carnyx."

"A what?" Anitha was describing the strange, loud metallic sounds that had deafened her during the episode.

"A carnyx is a metallic, usually bronze, wind instrument in the shape of a boar's head, sometimes, a serpent's head. It was used by iron-age Celts to rally for battles." Solomon sipped his hot chocolate. "This is really delicious Durga," he complimented.

"Thanks."

Stupefied, Anitha curled herself under her Mexican throw, a patchwork of riotous colours and motifs.

"I think I know what happened to you in the woods."

"You do?" Somehow, Anitha trusted what Solomon was about to say.

"You were given access to another realm from

another time for a purpose – the pregnant, black boar, the alarm of the carnyx…all are alive and thriving in that wood, coexisting with the 21st century but vibrating on a different level from ours."

This was all too much for Anitha. "Okay, okay. So what? What is the purpose of all this?" Agitated, she kicked a pink, silk cushion to the floor.

Gently, Solomon picked it up and placed it on his lap. "The spirit of that wood has made a connection with you on a profound level."

"Why?"

"You are called to battle."

Durga straightened up. "Battle?"

"Yes. That explains the carnyx you heard." He turned to Durga. "Do you have a copy of this month's parish magazine?"

Durga searched her basket of brochures, pamphlets, takeaway menus and magazines. "Here."

Leafing through the pages, Solomon pointed to page five. "Read."

Jaws dropped.

Jumping off her armchair, Durga angrily exclaimed, "This can't be happening!"

Rage surged hot and cold within Anitha. "Planning permission to build houses, a nursery, a playground and a carpark?" A rumble growled deep within the pit of her solar plexus. This explained her apocalyptic dreams – the end of this precious earth to serve an economic agenda. Anitha felt the pupils of her eyes slide. Tingling sensations slithered across her skin.

The woods. Ancient. Sacred. Her beloved woods. No. She will not let them destroy the woods. She understood now.

This was her destiny.

Her call to battle.

PART 2

CHAPTER NINE

October 31st – The Afternoon of All Hallows' Eve

It was the end of the day. Through the meandering corridors of the college, Anitha and Tilly strolled side by side like the best of friends. Rays of dimming sunlight washed across the stony spaces of the majestic, pointed arches and irregular, vaulted ceilings.

"Thanks for inviting me over tonight," Tilly said.

"My first time having anyone over," admitted Anitha.

Tilly threw her head back in a little laugh. "There is a first for everything."

"It's weird, isn't it? It's only been a few weeks and I feel...I feel like we..."

Tilly completed the sentence, "Are kindred spirits?"

"Yeah," Anitha agreed, softly, "yeah but I really appreciate you being in on this. Really. It's way too scary…too scary to attempt anything on my own but this is important to me and I know it is for you too."

"Most definitely." The reply was grim. "Anything to stop these greedy, kleptocratic maniacs from impoverishing the earth."

"You're right."

"And what about this boy?" There was a note of discontent in Tilly.

"Oh, Solomon? He's alright. I told you. He's not like the rest. He's different."

"Like us."

"Yup. And don't worry about the neighbour girl. She's leaving after dinner and I'll be with her for about an hour. I promised to help her with some personal issues and once I'm done, the three of us can discuss what we have to do."

"Save the woodland from grasping human hands." Tilly smiled. "Don't worry, Anitha, I have your back. Anyway, I'm off to collect my bag. I'm already packed. Meet you at the bus-stop."

"Cool." Anitha walked on, excited at the prospect of actually having a friend over for the night. Tilly was more than a friend. She was an ally, an ally in Anitha's destiny to protect the ancient Greenway woodland.

With Tilly by her side, Anitha felt confident and secure.

Abruptly, she stopped in her tracks. Something was calling her…it was not so much a call as a wail or even maybe a wrathful cry? She turned. Her gut feelings directed her eyes upwards. Looming down at her was a particular open-mouthed gargoyle with big, bulging eyes that pulsed subtly with pearly-sheened light. Its mouth stretched even wider. An unearthly keening moan unleashed furiously from its throat. Glued to the ground in shock, Anitha looked around at the other students who passed innocently by, oblivious to the creature above. In a split second, a shot of laser, like a beam aimed at her.

Winded, Anitha stumbled backwards. Books from her arms clattered to the ground. Two girls held her from falling and helped her with the books. "Are you okay?" one of them asked, concerned.

Nodding gratefully, Anitha breathed in and out. "I'm…I'm fine." She waited for them to disappear from sight and the corridor to be empty before looking upwards again.

The gargoyle glowered back but this time, set in stone.

CHAPTER TEN

Later that Evening – All Hallows' Eve

Outside, in the cold, darkening evening, the high-pitched squeals of children trick or treating filled the air. This year, Durga and Anitha had decided not to put up any Halloween decorations or give out treats. Anitha had also turned down the invitation to help out at the village hall party. After the nightmare of last year's Halloween, it was best this year was simple and quiet.

In the kitchen, Durga was clearing the leftovers from the dinner plates when Anitha entered with an empty lasagne dish. "Licked clean!" she beamed. "Thanks, Ma, for all this."

For dinner, Durga had prepared a gluten-free, brown rice lasagne with broccoli, cheese and garlic topped with slices of fresh, red chillies followed by a salad of black beans, rocket leaves, baby spinach and cherry tomatoes drizzled with olive oil, lemon juice and Himalayan pink salt. Back in the dining-room, the guests were discussing the commercialisation of Halloween.

Tilly barked, "Caricatures of witches are abominable...profit at the expense of bigotry.... dumbing down of All Hallows' Eve...if only these stupid children and their stupid parents knew what really happens during this night..."

Alhena defended Halloween. "That's a bit harsh. Children deserve the fun. There's nothing wrong with that."

Tilly snorted, "Oh please!"

Solomon remained silent.

"What really happens during Halloween?"Alhena approached the question with slight trepidation.

Tilly's voice descended to a low whisper. "You. Don't. Want. To. Know." Each word was enunciated slowly and dangerously.

Back in the kitchen, Durga and Anitha sensed the air chill. Hastily, Durga laid her freshly baked date and walnut flapjack onto a tray and pushed it into Anitha's hands. "It's time for dessert. Now."

* * *

An Hour Later
Alhena's Bedroom

"You three are up to something." Alhena was all washed and dressed for the night.

A blonde head popped in. "Is there anything else, my dear?" It was Beatrice, Alhena's nurse.

"No. I'm fine. Thanks, Bea."

"See you at eight in the morning. You girls have a nice evening."

Footsteps faded. "Are you ready?" Anitha watched Alhena's face for last minute changes.

"What is it with the three of you?"

"Huh?"

"The three of you...something's up."

"What makes you say that?"

Shrugging her shoulders, Alhena leaned against her propped pillows. "A feeling."

Amos and Levi came in to say goodnight. "That cat's been scratching on my porch all evening," Amos complained.

"YinYang?" Anitha said.

"Black and white? That's him." Levi eyed Amos. "It's cold out. We might just let him in tonight." He winked at Alhena. Amos did not seem amused but he relented.

Once they left, Alhena continued, "You're hiding something. All three of you…"

"I'm not here to discuss me."

"They like you, you know," Alhena giggled.

Puzzled, Anitha blinked her eyes, "What? Who?"

"Tilly and Solomon. They like you."

"They're friends. I hope so."

"Not like that, silly. They really like you. They're both cute but er…Tilly is a bit rude and domineering. There's something about her. She gives me the creeps. Solomon's sensitive."

"Thanks for the character critique. Now can we get back to you?" Anitha was beginning to get exasperated.

Suddenly, Alhena confronted the girl seated on her bed. "Who are you?"

The air stilled.

"One day, soon, I promise, I will let you in on the secret."

"Ah ha! Secrets! I knew it. I knew it since the day I first saw you…saw your eyes."

"Okay. You win but now, let me help you."

Alhena persisted. "Wait. Tell me. Why did you pick tonight? Tilly said something about Halloween… what really goes on?"

Anitha complied. "All Hallows' Eve is a sacred night. It is when the veils between the worlds are thin making it easy for spirits to slip through and roam freely."

"I've read about that."

"It is also an ideal time to connect with the dead… to communicate with those who have passed on to other realms."

"I see. So tonight, it will be easy to communicate with Regina. You think my dreams are linked to her?"

"I don't know."

"It's called the Vanishing Twin Syndrome, you know. I googled it. I practically sucked all the oxygen and nutrients out of her to feed myself. I ate the life out of my twin sis." Alhena mewled.

Kindly, Anitha touched Alhena's arm. "I can't explain your pain away, Ally, but I can help you connect with your dreams and from there, hopefully, you get an understanding of what to do with all this guilt and grief. You see, my dreams helped me to come to terms with what I had been feeling as a child. Why did I get to live and not my dad? For years, I suffered guilt and rage. I still do sometimes. I believed myself to be a curse. A jinx. It was my grandma who helped me navigate my dreams. She told me to listen to my dreams and see them without judgement. Your dreams don't solve problems or miraculously bring the dead back but…they will help you process whatever you are going through inside."

Feebly, Alhena said, "Okay. Thanks for sharing, Ani."

"Shall we?"

"What am I supposed to do?"

Grinning, Anitha edged closer. "Let me bite you."

CHAPTER ELEVEN

All Hallows' Eve

Back in Anitha's bedroom, three teenagers gathered, sipping hot turmeric lattes and finishing the last of the date and walnut flapjacks. Outside, night had fallen fast and cold. Anitha's naga blood throbbed hotly as she held the google print photograph of Kamini Smith in her hands.

Tilly mused, "The CEO of Home Front Development. It was easy getting downloads on her. She tweets a lot... the idiot puts her opinions online. Here are downloads on her company website." Tilly handed a few sheets of paper to Anitha and Solomon. "She's got her face and photos of her top management team on the website as well."

Anitha was curious. "How did you get into her Facebook?"

"Oh, please. I just clicked 'like' on her Facebook picture and she let me in. I created a fake account. It's not rocket science."

Solomon flipped through the copies. "If planning permission is given by the council, they will clear the woods in late spring."

"That's never going to happen." Inhaling deeply, Anitha leaned against the wall. "I have a plan." It was a plan she had been mulling over for some time. "We target Kamini Smith and her project team. If all they see, feel and smell is money and the luxury that is bought through exploitation of the earth, then we will bring the nightmare of their making to them. Let them see, feel and smell what I saw, felt and smelt."

Solomon's green eyes deepened to a grey. "How?"

"Through the best medium there is…dreams."

Tilly clapped her hands. "Brilliant! You mean, get into their heads and let them experience the apocalypse for themselves?" She bit into the last flapjack.

"Isn't that a form of psychic attack?" A guarded expression clothed Solomon's handsome face.

"No," Anitha pressed her lips in a tight line. "We are not attacking. We are merely showing them a glimpse of the end of the earth as it has been revealed to me. People watch films about this, don't they?"

"This is not a film," Solomon warned.

"No. It is the truth. Far more important than a stupid Hollywood blockbuster."

A touch of disquiet seeped into the room. Outside, the night had begun to drizzle and the almost full moon was hidden in sweeping shadows.

Grimly, Solomon said, "No casualties."

Tilly flicked a mirthless glance his way.

"I mean it. We slip into their dreams, channel your vision to them and then get out."

Anitha and Tilly looked at each other.

Solomon faced both of them squarely. "It is about freewill. You show them the truth and it is up to them to choose to evolve...or not."

Tilly's features slackened. "So...if they do not choose to evolve, then what? We just let the corporate vultures continue committing genocide against Mother Earth for their own personal agendas?"

"What this is about is bigger than us...way bigger than us...we might be powerful but we do not play judge and jury and we do not condemn anyone to death."

After some moments, Anitha spoke, "Agreed."

"Solomon rose to stretch his legs. He was seated at Anitha's study chair. "Good. Listen, I have to make a move soon. I promised Gran I'd be back before midnight but first, we have to decide when we do this...this dream transmission."

With averted eyes, Tilly suggested, "There is a dark moon in mid-November. That would be ideal to slip through dreams."

"Isn't a dark moon reserved for hexes...curses... psychic attacks and dark magick?" Solomon did not like the way this discussion was going. "Besides, there is a solar eclipse on that day."

Anitha interrupted. She was getting exhausted and just wanted to sleep. "Dark moons, eclipses...so what? If it is not our intention to cause harm, then that should make it safe."

Quietly, Solomon explained, "Intentions and deeds, no matter how pure and good and well-planned have a way of going wonky on eclipses..."

"Oh, just chill out, Sol!" Anitha threw her hands in the air. "We promised no casualties. Just meet us halfway, will you?" The night was dragging and she was tempted to crawl under her duvet and shut Tilly and Solomon up. Why did life have to be so complicated?

"What about the Winter Solstice?" Solomon suggested, giving it one last go.

Tilly intercepted before Anitha could say a word, "Too long to wait."

Ignoring Tilly, Solomon kept his eyes on Anitha. "Patience is a virtue. We can tap into the more positive energies of the Solstice."

Anitha shook her head. "Tilly's right. We have no time to waste. We do this on the November dark moon, solar eclipse and all. Whatever." She fixed her gaze on the tree branches swaying in the winds. "You don't have to be in on this, Sol if you feel otherwise. Freewill, remember?"

Hurt, Solomon was taken aback but he collected himself and offered, "I'm in but first, you have to transmit your dream into us."

"Fine. Pick a date." Inwardly, Anitha moaned. Was this night never going to end?

With her snow-white skin gleaming a porcelain pale, Tilly permitted a slight smile, "Why not now? After all it is All Hallows' Eve."

"Right. After that, Sol, you must leave, I have to sleep!"

Anitha returned to her bedroom with a basin of filtered water. "Now, hands in water, please." Tilly and Sol obeyed. "Water is a portal. It absorbs. It records. It remembers. Water is a great medium of transmission. My grandma said so."

CHAPTER TWELVE

All Hallows' Eve
Back in Alhena's Bedroom

It didn't hurt. The Bite. There was a slight sting where Anitha had bitten her just above the left ankle. Alhena did not have time to react.

She also did not see Anitha leave her bedroom but she did hear the door click shut. Alhena thought she was fast asleep but her mind was awake...

...to the fluid, black space she was floating in. Shadows swam through the ebb and flow of watery coils. A repetitive pulse drummed in repetitive beats soothing her initial fears. Listening closely, she heard a simultaneous, milder beat and she gasped...

Two heartbeats...

Rungs of pale, twisting cords resembling ladders, slithered with the sounds of the heartbeats, writhing, wriggling, winding and unwinding in a symbiotic dance. Incandescent, black pools of water reflected the strands as they sought to arrange and rearrange in interlocking, geometric patterns. Gradually, an apparition inked itself into formation.

Through the watery dunes of spirals, Alhena wept, "Regina!"

CHAPTER THIRTEEN

The sums were doing her head in. No matter how much she had worked on them, the algorithms confounded her. Crushing the papers, she disposed of them in the recycling basket and turned to her textbook. "I'll get to you later."

To the left of her study desk, sat her Medusa project. "Nothing has really changed much, has it, Medusa?" Anitha spoke aloud. "Patriarchy still continues to slut-shame you and smear you in books and movies and documentaries. Women and girls go through this every day. Can I really affect mainstream perception of you? From a monster that deserves to be feared and demonised to one worthy to be held as an icon of empowerment?"

Turning her gaze to the window, she saw the

steely-grey River Ouse meander quietly past. Willows swayed in the breeze and a family of starlings gathered to converse noisily. A couple of magpies flew past and perched on her window sill. In no mood to get any work done, Anitha lay on her bed, hoping a nap might help.

However, thoughts intruded on her mind. Firstly, she had not heard from Alhena. More than a week had passed since Anitha had offered to help her with her dreams on that All Hallows' Eve. Ally had not come around and Anitha was not about to harass her neighbour for updates. Secondly, she was excited about next week – The Dark Moon night…suddenly she jumped out of bed and snatched a file from her desk containing prints of Kamini Smith and Home Front Development.

Anger surged within her as she glanced through the pages again.

"Where are you off to?" Durga was about to leave for her afternoon shift at the nursery.

"A walk."

Durga eyed her daughter, suspiciously. "To the woods?"

"Yup."

"Have you finished your homework?"

"Almost…"

"Can we have a minute?"

"Now? What about?"

"I was meaning to talk to you about Mathilda…"

Anitha buttoned up her parka. "I know, she's cool right?"

"There is no right time to tell you this…put on your woolly hat…"

"Okay. Hurry up, Ma…"

"I can't see her."

"Huh?"

Durga repeated, cautiously, "I can't see her. She's wearing a cloak, a powerful glamour I am not familiar with. She must be some powerful witch."

"I've told you, Ma, she's got centuries old witch blood in her. Now, is that all?"

"The glamour is impenetrable. I am a naga and I am sensing something is amiss. She is hiding something…"

"Pimples? Warts? Excessive moles? A big nose?" Anitha was reaching for the door handle.

"It is not just me. Solomon seems to think so too…"

Anitha stopped short of swearing. "Solomon? Since when did he tell you?"

"He came by the weekend when you were in town with Mathilda. He wanted to share with us about his bloodline."

"So you and Sol are talking behind my back!"

Exasperated, Durga reproached her daughter, "Stop misreading what I am saying, young lady. Besides, I am your mother and it is my job to be concerned with who you are hanging out with."

"Oh! Now suddenly your maternal instincts kick in?" Anitha mocked, her lips twisting angrily. "From what I remember, you weren't really concerned about me last year when you conveniently had a meltdown and abandoned me in a foreign country…"

"That's cruel." Anitha's words hit Durga like an iron fist to her belly. "You were in Kerala, the home of your ancestors and you were safe in Amama's home, our family home."

"Whatever!" Anitha grabbed her set of keys. Tears stung her eyes. "You know what, Ma? For the first time I have a real friend, you ruin it. Thanks!"

"That's not fair, Anitha…"

The front door slammed shut.

CHAPTER FOURTEEN

Armed with maps, Kamini Smith and two of her team members from the Project Coordination Department ventured into the Greenway Woods to survey the land. They had been here more than a dozen times before and were familiar with the landscape. The day was cold, bright and clear. The chirping of birds rang merrily through the air. Light spilled generously through the branches of trees. Boots crunched noisily over ground thick with leaves.

It was going to be a challenge, the group discussed. Firstly, there were ongoing protests from the local and neighbouring villages gaining momentum further fuelled by environmental activists. Greenway Woods had not made national news yet but once the planning permission is approved, matters could turn messy. This possibility did not deter Kamini Smith. She possessed the money, clout and network of influential people as well as a corporate lawyer to handle any situation. 'To Hell with the environmentalists' was one of her many mottos that served her material success well.

Secondly, the woods were densely populated with ancient trees. It would take longer than ever to clear the land. The depth of the roots would pose problems. However, Kamini Smith was confident of the Norwegians she had hired to do the job. They had the most advanced equipment and came highly recommended. Dismissing the naysayers beside her, she said, "I'm turning left. Meet me by the river in about half an hour," and trudged off.

John slowed his pace so he could walk side by side with his colleague. "How are you holding up, May?"

May rubbed her eyes. She was sleepy. These days, she was always sleepy. No matter how tired she was, she would always wake up in the middle of the night, worrying. She worried about money, the monthly mortgage payments and the boys. Guilt tore her apart everyday as she wondered about giving her children the decent lifestyle they deserved. "I can't keep up with the mortgage payment John. I might have to look for a room to rent by the end of the year. I wake up sometimes with panic attacks and I frighten myself. I keep reminding myself to stay strong for the boys."

"Oh, May." John leaned against the willow tree and watched the river flow. It soothed his nerves. A part of him protested against the current project to build homes in this ancient woodland, but his hands were tied. This was his job and he needed the work.

May continued, "I have no choice. This winter, I have to choose between heating or food."

"I didn't realise it was that bad. I'm so sorry. I did appeal to Kamini, but you know what she's like, always defers any decision, which doesn't benefit her." John sighed. His blue eyes were still fixed on the gentle ripples of the water. "It is beautiful here. So peaceful."

May knelt to dip her fingers in the water. "What about you?"

"Sarah and I hardly speak anymore. Ted's medical bills are so expensive and going up all the time. I...we don't know what to do. He needs constant attention. Sometimes, sometimes, I just don't want to go back home."

"I'm so sorry," May looked at him sadly.

John looked up at a gathering of crows. "We could all do with a raise. As a team, we never shy away from putting in extra hours. I don't know now whether it was all worth it. I thought one was supposed to be rewarded for hard work…"

And then, there was the call of crows.

Kamini Smith stopped. Several crows had begun cawing collectively above her in the blue sky. For some reason she felt intimidated by their presence. They swerved in unison before flying off. A shape moved behind the massive trunk and buttress of an old beech. A golden-brown deer peeped out at her before galloping off into the thickening woods. Walking some yards ahead, her mind turned to the bank holiday weekend she and her family had enjoyed in the Greek islands. Plans for the Christmas break at the Alps were already set in motion…the log cabin, the sauna and skiing…

…hiss…

Kamini held her breath. Her face tightened.

hiss…

Her throat squeezed tight. A prickling weight sat on her chest. An absolute silence hit the woods – a hostile quiet. Her heart pounded.

hiss…

A wind lifted with a moan. Dustings of soil and damp, fallen leaves began to rise and drift around her boots. Higher and higher they floated, encircling her in slow motion. Lurching around, Kamini ran and ran losing all sense of direction before tripping on tangled roots and falling face forward on the base of a hunched yew tree. Old, gnarled roots uncoiled and like the knotty fingers of a witch, seemed to reach out and grip her and tear at her hot skin.

She let out a short, sharp scream.

CHAPTER FIFTEEN

Two Days Later

Done. Anitha felt relieved that she had finished the mathematical conundrum that took her ages to crack. There was just one more set of sums to complete before next week's deadline. Leaning back against her chair, she tapped her study table with her pen and gazed out of the window at the thin-lipped waning moon hanging silently in the evening sky.

The opportunity was too tempting to miss. Kamini Smith and her team in the woods. Some energy had come over her and she had found herself consciously channelling her naga pulse to connect to the spirit of the woods. After all, the woods had connected to her first when she was with Alhena before All Hallows' Eve.

To her delight, the channelling worked magick! The woods had come alive! And Kamini Smith was spooked!

It was only a spook. Nothing serious, Anitha defended herself. No harm done. In a matter of minutes, two of Kamini Smith's team had come and led her out of the woods. Surely now, Kamini Smith must realise that the woods was a living, breathing entity in its own right not some lump of monetary asset to be mined ruthlessly for human consumption.

Edged with a ghostly grey, the Ouse, a liquid sheet of rippling waves flowed past. Anitha's fingertips tingled as she recalled her power. Secretly, she was pleased. The rush was exciting. The high, exhilarating...

The doorbell rang.

"I'll leave you two be," Durga smiled at Solomon. "You sure I can't do you a hot drink?"

"No thanks Durga."

"Fine," Durga left the bedroom door ajar before returning downstairs to her willow-weaving. She was in the process of weaving coasters to gift friends for Christmas. It took her mind off the cruel words Anitha had spoken recently. Her daughter had apologised but the hurt still lingered. The guilt, heavier. She missed her husband. Badly. Anitha missed the dad she never had. Just as badly. The torment – never ending.

Solomon looked around the bedroom. "So, how have you been?"

"Busy." Anitha distracted herself with tidying her textbooks and papers.

"It's the dark moon next week."

"Yup. The big night."

"That was some powerful, apocalyptic vision you transmitted to us on All Hallows' Eve."

"Yup." The tidying continued.

"Hey, I came by the other day to talk to you… about me…"

"Yeah. My mum told me. She also told me what the two of you think of Tilly."

Refusing to stray from his reason for the visit, Solomon sat on Anitha's bed with its sage-coloured sheet and fixed his green eyes on her brown ones. "You and I are one…"

"I figured."

"Just like you, I am a descendant of the serpent bloodline. I am the descendant of the Midgard Serpent."

Anitha stopped her organising and paid attention.

"Just like your ancestry, mine is relegated to myth and bestsellers…"

"Okay. Tell me more."

"It's all online, you know." Solomon drew a half-smile as Anitha rolled her eyes. "Alright, alright…my ancestor, the Midgard Serpent, the Jormungand is the offspring of the Norse God Loki and the giantess Angrboda."

Widening her eyes, Anitha chirped, "I've heard of Loki, the trickster god! Wow!"

"Yeah, he was a wildcard, a trouble maker as history would have it."

"Wrong side of the DNA," joked Anitha.

"Black sheep of the family," chuckled Solomon. "Well, anyway, to cut the story short, Jormungand plays a pivotal role in bringing about the end of the world. The old corrupt order with the old gods will be destroyed and a new symbiotic order will take its place. No more wars. No more hostilities – only harmony between humans, the earth and the heavens."

"Is that even possible?" muttered Anitha as flashes of her apocalyptic visions jabbed her mind.

"Tragically, in the process, my ancestor will perish."

A moth fluttered in, fluttering about before resting in a corner of the ceiling just above the bed. A respectful pause settled in the bedroom. Solomon resumed his narrative, "My mum found out about my dad's bloodline. She witnessed it…"

Anitha interrupted, "Let me see, she accidentally stumbled upon him shedding."

Nodding, Solomon stared at the moth. "She went mad. Literally. She's been in a private facility in London for years. My dad's parents raised me. Grandpa died a couple of years ago. It's just me and Gran now."

"Where's your dad?"

"Somewhere in Norway; he sends a birthday card each year. He had left Ebony behind for me."

Tears sprung in Anitha's eyes. "I…I'm sorry about her." The image of her cousin flinging Ebony against the slipway rocks made her shudder.

"She comes to me in my dreams. Sometimes, I hear her purr." Solomon's eyes glistened. Minutes passed. He rose. "Hey, would you like to take a walk with me down the riverbank?"

"A walk?" Dabbing her eyes with the sleeve of her sweater, Anitha declined. "It's cold and dark. Besides, I have maths to finish and my Medusa project…"

"Do them later. It's only half-five. Come on. Wrap up warm."

The riverbank was soft, wet and muddy. Softly, waving willows rustled in the shadows of the descending evening. An owl hooted in the sycamore tree. Ducks quacked low in a hidden mound further down the trail.

"What's your mum's name?" Anitha pulled her red, woollen hat down her ears.

Close beside her, Solomon walked with hands in the pockets of his jacket. "Ingrid."

"Your dad?"

"Ivan."

Soft puffs of breeze blew. The grey, silvery Ouse reflected the gleam of the sickle moon. Anitha could sniff Sol's cologne in the air. A hint of wood and herbs. He was close. Too close. He was tall. Too tall.

"I was meaning to ask you..."

Detecting a nervous tone, Anitha's heart skipped a beat. She heard the squelch of the mud-thick earth beneath their boots. "Ask away."

"Would you like to go out with me...sometime..."

"We are out...you asked me, remember, ten minutes ago? You dragged me out of my warm, dry bedroom..."

Solomon slipped her a shy look. "I mean like the movies or...a cafe...maybe a meal somewhere healthy?"

Once more, the owl let out a hoot, flapped its wings and soared across the blackened river. The darkening evening was drowsy with cold droplets of mist that skimmed along their faces.

After a moment of reservation, Anitha said, "Maybe when we have got past the psychic mission for the Greenway!"

CHAPTER SIXTEEN

The November winds rushed coldly against her face as she turned into the close. This was the beginning of her coming into her own new skin. Saving the woods was her first challenge. Romantic feelings could not be allowed to obstruct her path to a Higher Call. Her new skin had blessed her with a new lease of life, a meaning, a profound purpose that went beyond the mundane…

"Anitha! Ani!" It was Alhena, waving to her from her porch. "Can we talk?"

In Alhena's dining room, Amos served two generous slices of Victoria sponge cake and mugs of steaming hot chocolate topped with marshmallows. "Enjoy, ladies."

"Thanks, sir. It smells gorgeous!" Anitha was feeling slightly peckish and warmed her hands around the mug.

"Oh, please, call me Amos. There is no need for formalities. Even Ally calls me Amos."

Laughing, Anitha agreed and commented on how beautiful the dining-room was with its rosewood table and chairs, crystal wall lamps and an ornately designed, five-foot, gold gilded mirror that hung grandly near the doorway. The carpet was a wine-red woven piece with patterns of deserts, olive trees, birds and synagogues.

"I purchased that from an old flea market back in Israel. It must be over three decades old." Amos noticed Anitha was admiring it.

"I could sleep on it," Anitha bent to stroke its luxuriously, silky texture.

"Just once. Why not?" Amos joked, his eyes, twinkling. "Anyway, I'll leave you two girls. I'll be busy upstairs if you need anything." He ruffled his niece's hair fondly and promptly exited.

Alhena sipped her drink. "I saw you leave with Solomon." She tiptoed on the words.

"Just a walk." A meow made Anitha turn. "YinYang!"

The cat leapt on Alhena's blanketed knees. Grinning, Alhena buried her face in YinYang's fur and said, "It's official – I am his. Amos wasn't too keen at first but Levi got one of his friends to build a cat flap. He's free to come and go."

Anitha offered YinYang some crumbs from her hand. "I'm glad he has a home now. He's been a stray for a while."

The girls fussed over the cat before he decided he had had enough. He jumped off Alhena's knees and sprawled on the carpet. "That makes Amos nervous. Really nervous!"

"I'm sure. It's clearly a beautiful, sentimental piece."

Lazily, YinYang rolled about before padding himself out of the room. Alhena forked a bit of her cake and popped it into her mouth. "I'm sorry I didn't get back to you after that night…"

"No worries."

Alhena breathed deeply. "Who are you, Ani? Or… what are you? You hypnotised me and left…jeez. Who does that?"

"In time, Ally, in time. I promise. I just wanted to help but I've got too much on my mind now and I'm not ready to explain myself."

"I have to say, though. I slept well. I can't remember the last time I did." Alhena took another helping. "I admit – you scare me…the first time I saw you, your eyes…they changed colour…then you held my hands… and then the dream…I don't understand any of it…"

Anitha broached the subject gently, "The dream, Ally. Tell me." The hot chocolate was delicious.

"Yes, the dream. It was like being awake and dreaming at the same time. It was like being in another world but I remembered this place. It was the place before I was born. I was back in my mother's womb and, and..." Alhena paused, staring into space.

"And?"

"Regina was there. With me. I knew it was her. There were no words. I felt her. I felt her love." Alhena began crying. "I realised I was holding on to her death in my dreams. I was not letting her go. I am my own worst nightmare. There were no monsters and demons. I was haunting myself. My guilt...I had given it so much life..." Her sobbing increased. Upstairs, Amos was running the bath and listening to music.

"Do you still dream?" Anitha offered a tissue from her pocket.

"Yes. The dreams continue on and off but I am not scared anymore. I have a feeling she wants to be free, free from my guilt."

"That can't be a bad thing, Ally. When you free her, you free yourself but she will always be in your heart. You felt the love. The love can't go away. I know. I feel my dad's presence sometimes, when I'm walking or just before bedtime. It's funny but I never knew him when he was alive but he is here. With me. I don't expect anyone to understand."

Alhena blew her nose and agreed. "You are right. You see Ani, with my twin dead, my mum's suicide, my dad gone…I tried to kill myself because I told myself, why not? After all my life was over before I was even born and now, I can never walk again…but this dreaming Ani, this dreaming, it's done something to me!"

Anitha finished her hot chocolate. "It will take time, Ally. These dreams will not solve your problems or create miracles, but they will continue to help you in ways you do not know yet."

"This dreaming – it was as if I was in touch with something or some force that was bigger than me, bigger than this life…I don't know how to begin to explain it. I felt unstuck, rewired or something."

"No need to explain. I get it. Just flow with the dreams. You will be okay, trust me?"

Alhena looked at the grandfather clock. "Bea, my nurse is coming in a short while to help prepare me for bed. I wish I could talk to you more." She pushed a box towards Anitha. "Amos packed a slice for your mum."

"Thanks. I'll make a move. Listen. We're neighbours. Don't be a stranger." She hugged Alhena.

"Hey, Ani, I don't know what you are and you still scare me a bit, but thanks anyway!"

PART 3

CHAPTER SEVENTEEN

Greenway Woods
Mid-November – Solar Eclipse – Almost 3 pm

Like the rise of a black tide, shadows of darkness waved across the golden sun. Squirrels and rabbits scrambled into their holes. The last of the remaining leaves ceased to rustle. Winds dropped. Birds hushed.

And day became night.

Fog shimmered in watery, translucent ripples. Overlapping, incoherent mutterings weaved through the veiled trees and murmuring river. The crick crack of twigs and fallen branches echoed in deliberate pauses. Anitha sensed a presence in the woods. A presence of long, long ago. That was why she was here. To re-connect to the spirit of the woods for the spirit of the woods emboldened her. It nourished her naga blood and blessed her with the divine right to defend the woods.

She was the Chosen Warrior.

A snort and a grunt made her turn her head. She held her breath. Around her, the air stilled and the iridescent fog thinned, dissolving into strokes of talismanic wisps. From behind a worn-out yew, the black boar surfaced, heavily pregnant and wildly fearless in her commanding pose.

Mesmerised, Anitha whispered, "I see you see me…"

And the metallic clang of the carnyx tore across the woods, in a deafening, feverish pitch sounding the cry for battle…

CHAPTER EIGHTEEN

Several Hours Later
Dark Moon – Almost 3 am
Anitha's Home – Living-Room

The night was laced with frost with the temperature dipping to the lowest of the year. Outside, the black sky was erased of stars and moon. A lone, shriek of an owl sliced through the thick, quiet of the pre-dawn air.

Anitha, Mathilda and Solomon sat in a circle, cross-legged. The living-room was warm with the heat of the electric fireplace. They were ready for The Dreamtime. A sense of anxious anticipation seeped through the space. Bearing a big, metallic bowl filled with pure water, Durga came in and positioned it in front of the teens. Then she lit a candle and secured it on the candlestick holder at the hearth. Finally, she switched off the lights. A dim, glow of orange flickered and then settled, casting shadows on the walls.

Durga sat outside the circle for she was The Watcher. Her task was to keep a vigilant eye on the three. "Amama is also keeping watch," she turned to Anitha. "The first sign of trouble, she's rousing all three." Then Durga addressed the circle. "Only an hour. No more. You will sense when the time is almost up. I will wake you into consciousness." Her gaze directed at Anitha and Solomon. "Remember, your venomous dose must be just enough to induce a lucid dream. And you, Mathilda," Mathilda's blue eyes landed attentively on The Watcher, "you will spell them to sleep."

"I'm pretty adept with rhyming, I'm told..." Mathilda flashed a grin.

Anitha stifled a giggle but neither Durga nor Solomon found it amusing. The clock began chiming. The candle flame stilled.

"Right, you know your chosen sleepers. So, we begin." Durga placed the internet pictures of Kamini Smith, her team managers, a select few of the Norwegian loggers and builders into the bowl of water. She motioned the three young people before her to immerse their hands, wrist deep into the bowl. "Close your eyes, take deep, slow breaths and...connect..."

Anitha shimmered in a corner of the dark bedroom. Kamini Smith was fast asleep but the man in pyjamas next to her was awake and typing on his laptop. Sheaves of papers were strewn on the floor and on the bed. An empty bottle of beer lay on the rug. This was not foreseen.

Irritated, she flicked her forked tongue and crocodile-like, slithered on all fours to his side of the bed where she paused for a second before nipping him lightly on his left ankle. Startled, he jumped a bit and scratched the area. The effect was immediate. His eyelids drooped, his arms slipped to his sides and drowsiness set in. Soon he was asleep.

Noiselessly, Anitha picked up his laptop and put it on the floor, before sliding to the woman beside him.

Anitha, Mathilda and Solomon were on the floor. They were breathing deeply and occasionally twitching. They were in astral mode. Durga laid blankets on each of them and poured herself a cup of coffee from the pot on the coffee table. Her eyes were on them. As the clock ticked, she waited for the hour to arrive.

CHAPTER NINETEEN

Hiss…

Her eyes snapped open. Kamini clenched her duvet close to her chin. The bedroom was dark and Jim was snoring beside her. She must have been dreaming and suddenly woke up.

"Hiss…"

Her blood ran cold. No. It couldn't be. Not again. Not in her home. Maybe she had had too much wine. That's it. Then she heard a sound. Like a shuffle. She propped herself up against the headboard and scanned the room. Rats? Mice? She clutched and squeezed Jim's arm but he was fast asleep. Kamini blinked and widened her eyes at a skulking figure beneath her massive, curtained window. There was a glint emanating from the smallish figure, lending a faint suggestion of a slim, human, feminine form. Something did not seem right. The hairs on her arms stiffened. Her heart thumped like the way it did in the woods.

"Hiss…"

A scream lodged itself in her throat. Frantically, Kamini Smith shook her husband, but he continued sleeping heavily.

Draped in mercurial, glassy scales, Anitha launched herself sinuously upon the CEO. She hovered close to the petrified, white face and flicked her undulating, forked tongue at her. Venom dripped.

"Wha…what are…what are you?" squeaked Kamini.

With golden-gleaming eyes, Anitha spat venom into her mouth and hissed, "The Apocalypse."

CHAPTER TWENTY

Kamini winced at the intense burning pain in her mouth. Her sight blurred. Numbness set in her face and body. Her breathing laboured as she kept falling and falling into black space...

Before her lay a wasteland. A landscape of emptiness. The air was thick with chemical smells and industrial smoke. She coughed and choked. People walked by, absorbed in communicating to their attached gadgets, not noticing her. Many were thin and gaunt. Others were dangerously skeletal in appearance but all shared the same hollow-eyes. Sounds of machines, vehicles and drones whirred all around. Disoriented and terrified, Kamini Smith screamed for help but no one heard. Where was she? What was happening to her?

"Hiss..."

"*Get away from me!*" she begged hoarsely, spinning around aimlessly before her knees buckled and she fell into the blackness again...

She found herself somewhere else. There were neat rows of houses with garages and in the near distance, a playground and a nursery. The unfolding scene reminded her of the Greenway Housing Project plan. Oblivious to Kamini Smith, people, mostly women, unsmiling, stressed and agitated, went past in a hurried manner with children in tow. They too were glued to their gadgets. Not a single tree nor flower was in sight. The grass was fake on lawns and CCTV cameras were everywhere. Tall, metallic structures of masts littered the residential area.

"*Hiss...*"

A girl covered in shiny, snake scales stood a few yards away from her. Her forked tongue flicked out. Jerking backwards, Kamini Smith clumsily landed on her backside. Her limbs had seized up and sweat drenched her from head to toe.

Suddenly, the snake-girl spoke, in a silky tone. "*This is the earth of the future. The earth of your making.*"

Reeling backwards, Kamini wheezed, "*Leave me alone!*" Words tangled in her dry throat.

"*How can I?*" The monster continued. "*When you and people like you mine the earth for your own agenda. My kind refuse to sit by and simply watch."*

Terror washed over Kamini Smith. "Your kind?"

Golden eyes pulsed. Silvery-glassy scales vibrated. Fiery sparks shot through the flicking forked tongue.

"Please…please…" Kamini Smith whimpered, her sweating body, shivering. "I have children, they need me…they're so young," she howled. She could not feel her legs anymore.

The unearthly creature scoffed. "Birds have young too. Trees have young too. Insects have young too. What do you and those like you care? And when your children grow up, will they care?"

"Don't you dare speak of my children!"

"Hiss…" the snake-girl taunted.

Recognition dawned on Kamini. "You! It was you! In the woods!" she let out a strangled screech. "What are you? You freak!"

Unperturbed, the unnatural thing proclaimed imperially, "I am The Keeper of the Woods. A Guardian of the Earth."

Kamini Smith gasped. Images of her children entered her mind – their laughter, their call to her, 'Mummy! Mummy!' She felt their cuddles and kisses. Tears poured down her cheeks. Scenes of happy family gatherings flashed intermittently. Holidays of past, present and those to come throbbed enticingly before her. Rage built inside her belly as she spat at the creature who threatened her happiness. "Go...to...hell...!"

The concrete ground quaked and split. Slimy white liquid oozed from the cracks emitting a chemical stench. Buildings swayed side to side before collapsing like a house of cards.

Her head spun, blurring her vision. Her breathing became increasingly testing as she bent over and vomited. Her mouth was burning badly. Wildly, Kamini Smith wept, "I just want to go home!"

"At least you have a home..."

The snake girl was closer to her.

"The woods is home to wildlife. Where will they go when you raze their home? Their families will end with them."

Kamini Smith grabbed a pile of sticks from the soft earth and desperately flung it at the beastly girl before her. "Get away from me!"

In that moment, a shroud of mists descended. A cacophony of cackling incantations burst through the veil of the dreamtime. Through the chilling vapours, sibilant hisses echoed. An incorporeal force pushed the snake girl to the far side as she landed with a thump on her back. She was stunned.

Kamini thrashed around while gasping for air. There were trees. Tall trees, short trees, young trees, old trees...sturdy *trees, rotting trees…even dead trees and their stumps… all breathing and closing in on her…and screeching… screeching at her…from above, birds, their beaks dipped in grave silence, swerved in synchronised lines before swooping down and smacking her repeatedly with their wings.*

Screaming, Kamini flailed her arms, helplessly. "No…ooo…ooo!" Saliva frothed from her singed mouth. She jerked in convulsions before expelling her final breath.

And the forest eclipsed into a blackness.

CHAPTER TWENTY-ONE

Birdsong drifted serenely through the dreamy, silver-edged mists as pale sun streaks slipped through the clouds of the grey-blue sky. The trees had retreated and the forest was back to its natural state.

In a crumpled heap, Kamini Smith lay motionless with her eyes open and mouth apart. Her once wavy, light brown hair was now white. Beneath a young yew, sat Anitha. Her scales were cold and wet. It was not supposed to end this way, she thought miserably. Unable to repress her hot streaming tears, she bawled, "What have I...!"

"What have you done?" a roar reverberated through the woods. Birds took flight. The earth rumbled. Anitha jumped up. Her bones rattled. She recognised Solomon's green eyes, but this time he was embossed in serpentine scales of sun-gold and sea-blue. He was simply glorious to

behold and he was tall, very, very tall. Literally a giant. A giant snake. "What have you done?" His voice was a primal deep, an all time low, growling hiss.

"I don't know how this...this happened..." words gargled in Anitha's throat as she noticed Solomon's eyes burn an amber red. He was mad. At her. "The forest, this was my dream...I don't know how it came alive... and took over...I swear, Sol, I didn't mean to hurt her. You must believe me." All of a sudden, she felt puny. Her knees wobbled as Solomon towered above her. "How did you...what are you doing in my dreamtime?" Cautiously, Anitha stepped back as Solomon's golden green eyes crackled with pin-prick lights.

His enormous webbed feet were built to squash her like a bug. Suddenly, Anitha sprinted. Solomon frightened her. How did he enter into her dreamtime? How dare he? She heard his thunderous feet stomp, stomp, stomp behind her. She spied the heavily sagging coven of yews and dashed towards the river. She did not know why she was heading that way. Just gut instinct. She skidded to a halt.

The river. It was bubbling and swirling and spluttering about. Like a witch's brew, it churned the ripples into a single wave that lifted and soared. Up and up it rose. Solomon ceased giving chase. Like Anitha, he was dumbfounded. Fretful winds whined and whipped *about as shadows congregated within the lone, surging wave to form a serpentine hood. Anitha's breath bolted in her chest.*

Without warning the tsunami wave of the river came crashing down on both the teenagers and dragged them into its watery depths.

CHAPTER TWENTY-TWO

The Hospital

Gargoyles hovered before her, keeping guard. Their feral, ancient features were not menacing anymore.

Not here.

Beneath the grand oak, piglets squealed as Mother Boar fussed despite sheer exhaustion. Trees sighed gustily. The wooded air, laden with the scents of moss and mud and leaves and blooms, soothed the nest of nerves in her belly.

All was well.

Here.

CHAPTER TWENTY-THREE

The Hospital
First Week of December

Her eyes fluttered open. Concerned whispers eddied about. A chemical stink made her retreat into the darkness.

"Go away." They did not hear. "Leave." They still did not hear. Faint outlines of familiar, talking faces merged and dissolved...

...into gauzy textures as pellucid-winged snakes flitted casually, their scales glinting a myriad of hues. The gargoyles and pigs and the woods and the comforting smells of the earth returned. This time, she was dipping her toes in the cold, fresh river.

Suddenly, the dramatic, metallic call of a trumpet

shattered the serenity of the forest. Trees shook. The river paused in its flow. The forest disappeared leaving her in a fog of dense, white space. The trumpeting persisted. Clang! Clang! Clang! He…what did he call it? That glorious giant of a shining snake…carnyx! That's it! Carnyx!

This remembering hurt her head badly. Her ears ached as the Clang! Clang! Clang! reached a heightened, alarming pitch. She felt the rush of her blood. The drum of her heart. Her body shuddered.

And a wall of sterilised air hit her nostrils.

CHAPTER TWENTY-FOUR

The Hospital

Anitha swallowed the last of her plain porridge. She felt hemmed in by the presence of the visitors but not wanting to appear ungrateful, she smiled and went along with the chatter. Nurse Kate entered the ward, greeted everyone pleasantly and took Anitha's temperature. After an approving look, she scribbled some notes on the papers attached to her clipboard and left wishing all a good day.

"So," Durga resumed, "after Christmas, you'll be spending Saturdays in college attending remedials for the lessons you have missed. Everything's been arranged with your tutors. The deadlines for your projects have been extended till the first week of January. They are extremely supportive of you and send you their best wishes."

Anitha wanted to sink back into her pillows and bury herself under the duvet. Two weeks. She had been in a coma for about two weeks. How did that happen?

"She's their star pupil," Mathilda teased, kindly. "They miss her."

Anitha handed the porridge bowl back to her mother.

Amos noted, "It's good to see you have a healthy appetite. We've made you some tasty soup for later. It's an old recipe from my great-grandmother. When I was sick, my mother used to make me this soup. It did the trick."

Durga received the red flask from Amos. "Aw, that's so sweet of you. Thank you."

Levi added, "We didn't forget you, Durga. We saved a portion for you."

Durga's eyes glistened. "You shouldn't have but I must admit, I haven't been cooking much lately."

"We figured." Levi offered a side hug. His neighbour had lost a considerable amount of weight and shadows circled under her eyes. Even her hair was noticeably greyer.

Alhena manoeuvred Jag to get closer to Anitha. "Here." She handed a cardboard painting to her friend.

"What's this?" Anitha stared and then gasped, "Oh my god, Ally! This is gorgeous!"

Everyone strained to have a look. It was a painting of Anitha, intently observing the river in the woods. The colours were vivid and Anitha's intense, contemplative expression was perfectly captured in Ally's colourful brushstrokes.

Alhena gushed at the compliments about the painting. "That day when we went to the woods, Ani, I saw you in this exact pose and committed it to memory. You, the woods and the river inspired me…"

"You certainly did capture the best of my daughter, Alhena. My goodness. You have a gift. I'll get this framed."

"Really? You will frame it? Gosh. Thanks."

Amos kissed his niece on the head. "I'm so proud of you, sweetheart. It's a masterpiece."

"Amos, please." Alhena was suddenly overwhelmed by all the attention.

Levi murmured appreciatively, "No, he's right, Alhena. It's beautiful."

Even Tilly was astounded. "The willows seem to be actually sweeping in the winds! And the yew – their roots! Coiling like live snakes! Genius!"

Durga and Anitha shot Tilly a warning glance.

"Thank you, Ally. I don't know what else to say.

This is just beautiful." Anitha hugged her neighbour. "Thank you."

"Thank *you*." Winking, Alhena placed Anitha's left hand on Jag's armrest.

No shadows swirled in tight knots. Jag felt more like Ally herself. There were only faint traces of Regina left. That was fine. Normal. After all they had been twins in the womb. That must be honoured. Accepted.

Amos, Levi and Alhena chatted for a little longer before saying their goodbyes and promised another visit in a couple of days.

Once they left, Durga wore a serious expression. "Just to keep you updated – Kamini Smith is in a coma. She suffered a stroke."

Anitha's heart was brick-heavy.

"Plans for the Greenway Housing Project fell through." Tilly perched on the bed and put her right hand on Anitha's lap. "Many of her staff members have resigned. Even the Norwegian loggers are planning to return to Norway." Her eyes shone a sea-blue. "There is a chance that Home Front Development will fold." She sounded chirpy.

This irked Durga. "Kamini Smith is in a coma, Mathilda. This was not supposed to happen."

Shrugging her shoulders nonchalantly, Tilly ignored the castigation. "Well, it did and the forest is safe. That is all I'm bothered about. Anyway, I best make a move."

"Thanks for coming." Anitha reached out to Tilly. They hugged.

When Tilly left, Durga bristled, "What's wrong with that girl?"

"Leave her be, Ma…er…Ma, where is Sol?"

"He's in London, visiting his mother. He'll be back before Christmas. Listen, Ani, your Amama told me to tell you that the reason why she had to intercept and retrieve you and Solomon from your dreamtime was because…"

"Whoa! Wait! Wait! Amama did that? That big killer wave!"

"Amama did not do that. She was the wave."

"Are you kidding? She was that river-wave whatever that almost killed Sol and I!"

"Now you're really overreacting." Durga waved her hands in the air. "That must be the human in you. Stop whining. How did you think you and Solomon were going to get out? Both of you were not in a fit state of mind."

"She's a scary granny."

"She's been worse. Trust me. Anyway, I was saying – your grandma sensed an interloping energy in your dreamtime. Not in Mathilda's and Solomon's. Only in yours. This uninvited energy caused the unintended consequence."

Anitha curled into a ball and slid under her duvet. "What are you saying, Ma? I don't have any control over my dreams or my mind? That I'm weak and easily manipulated? That Tilly and Sol are better at being who they are?"

"Stop that."

"No wonder I was in a coma. I'm useless at this astral, dreamtime thing. I'm never going to do this again! Ever! I'm a lousy naga!" Anitha cried, silently.

"There, there," Durga soothed her daughter. Gently, she brushed her soft hair with her fingers.

Anitha pretended to fall asleep so her mother would leave. When she was finally alone, thoughts tumbled in her head. Nobody knew she had connected to the spirit of the woods on that solar eclipse afternoon. Had she unleashed a force or maybe permitted one through? Did a spirit latch on to her from the woods and follow her back home? She had no answers.

Sol was right about eclipses. They were dodgy!

CHAPTER TWENTY-FIVE

January – The First Week of the New Year

Durga opened the front door. The moon was complete against the unobscured, black sky. She blinked in disbelief as its smooth, pale beam slipped right through Mathilda's milk-hued skin, casting a watery, wavering effect upon the night visitor. Snowflakes drifted lightly to the ground.

"Thanks for letting me stay the weekend, Miss Durga."

"Come in. Anitha is in her room."

Mathilda grinned as Durga composed herself, watching the tall, spirit-like girl enter her home like the chill of the snow wind.

* * *

Anitha's Bedroom

Seeing Medusa
I see you
You did not turn me to stone.
Your untamed crown of slithering locks
shed the Light of Wisdom and Healing.
Whisper your hisses of Divine Counsel
as you churn the Waters of Change
dissolving the lies of his-story
rebirthing Her-Story.
Weaver of the yet unwoven,
Queen of the Hidden
Oldest of Old,
O Medusa,
I see you
and you did not turn me to stone.

"What a superb way to close your project," Tilly complimented. She reread the poem, this time, aloud. "I've not read your work but I'm sure you'll get an A." This did not cheer her friend up. Anitha appeared worn out and unenthusiastic. "What's wrong?"

In a dispirited tone, Anitha shared, "Nightmares, Tilly, nightmares that woman comes to me, most nights!" she took a sip of her hot chocolate.

"Who? And what nightmares?"

"Kamini Smith. She's haunting me in my dreams. I'm losing sleep."

"How long have you been having these nightmares?"

"For a week now."

It took a few minutes before Tilly spoke. "It's crazy isn't it, that someone like you, basically a good person with good intentions who caused unintended consequences should have to endure bad dreams while those who commit wilful crimes for profit and power sleep without a care and wake up energetic the next day to commit more crimes."

"Tell me why?"

"Conscience."

"Conscience?"

Tilly began to unzip her haversack. "Conscience. When you have one, it bugs you. When you don't have one, you do what you will."

"So, you think it is not Kamini Smith who is haunting me in my sleep but me myself? My conscience?"

Tilly removed a beautifully bound big, fat book and handed it to Anitha. "That's just my perspective."

"What's this? Oh my god! I've never seen anything like this! It's gorgeous!" Anitha balanced the heavy book in her hands but feeling its weight, decided to lay it on the bed instead.

"It's a family heirloom and written in old German."

Anitha traced her fingers on the stunning illustration of the book cover – tall trees with intricately knotty roots shrouded in shadows with overhanging mists. The pregnant moon shone light upon miniature flitting spectres. Thin, pointy and winged, they glanced sideways at her with slanting, upswept features as though indicating she has been seen.

"They are the fae," Tilly explained.

"The fae? Like in fairies?"

"The fae of the forest. The unseen species that inhabit the natural world. The fae are rapidly dwindling because of human activities."

Anitha could not take her eyes off the pages. "But… what's in the book?" She was genuinely impressed and curious.

"This is The Book of Hex."

Shocked, Anitha exclaimed, "Hex? Isn't that…like a curse?"

"And why not? This is one of three books handed down for centuries through the bloodline…"

Anitha completed her sentence, "Of your ancestor, Flora, the witch?"

"Yes," Tilly proudly proclaimed. "Knowledge and Power granted to Flora and her descendants by the Goddess Holda Herself."

"This is really cool."

After a quiet moment, Tilly moved closer to Anitha on the bed. "You should too, you know."

"What?

"Create your own book."

"Huh?"

"Your own Power Book."

Anitha listened. "Go on…"

"In your own, personal Power Book, you can include details of your journey so far, your dreams, good, bad and prophetic, your experiences especially in this first dreamtime…"

"Even if…"

"Yes. Be honest. Include the unintended consequence. It's a learning curve. Just because we have unique bloodlines does not mean we don't make mistakes. You can also note the advice and pertinent information given to you by your gran and your mum. And don't forget your poems. This Medusa piece is perfect."

"I wrote one last year as well. My gran said with time, my naga blood will inspire me to compose serpent songs. In Malayalam, they are called nagapattu. It is a tradition in Kerala in many families that still hold on to the serpent faith. Festivals are held yearly and nagapattus are sung to and danced to as well. Gran says some of these compositions are centuries even thousands of years old."

"There you go. Your own serpent songs. Your own Power Book. Your own Book of Naga."

"I like the sound of that." Anitha continued to admire The Book of Hex.

"I'm a little tired. Is it okay if I take a shower and go to bed?"

"Go ahead. Hey, Tilly, thanks…"

"We're kindred spirits. This is what we do."

"May I hold on to this book till I fall asleep? I'm not ready to go to bed just yet."

"Sure. Good night, then." Tilly closed the door behind her as Anitha returned to the Book of Hex.

3 AM

Clawed nails scraped and scratched the window pane. A blanched face with a deadpan expression pressed against the glass. An unearthly glint bounced off the cadaverous features. The stink of rotting flesh permeated in the air. In sinister, slow-motion, thin lips stretched back tightly in a botched, clownish leer.

Kamini Smith chuckled wheezily, "I see you, little girl. I see you."

Anitha sprang to her feet and rushed to the guest

room. Tilly was not in the bed. Anitha's mind reeled in confusion and fear. Her throat closed up.

"Anitha?" Tilly was behind, cool and white like porcelain. "Are you okay?"

"No…no…wh…where were you?"

"I needed the loo. You're shaking. Sit down." The girls sat on the guest bed. "Th…that…was…not my conscience!" Anitha floundered as she recalled the nightmare. "That was not my conscience bugging me! It was…it was a…a…monster!"

Tilly pacified her friend. "Shhh…we don't want to wake your mum up."

"I'm telling you, Tilly, this…this was not like the other dreams. This…this thing was…was…demonic."

"Okay, okay." Patiently, Tilly waited as Anitha cried on her shoulders. "I do not disagree. Maybe, maybe that was a demon in your dream."

"You believe me?" Anitha sobbed a little less.

"What you witnessed was the real face of evil – those who currently impose their will upon this earth for their personal benefit. In your dream, you saw all that greed, power and selfishness in that one ugly face."

"So?" Anitha was still trembling. Her hands were cold.

Tilly inhaled. "Listen, Ani, your gran is right. You

have a call, a destiny that is far superior than just living an ordinary human life."

"What has that got to do with this…this demon? How can I get rid of this nightmare?"

Tilly put her right arm around Anitha's shoulders. "See, Ani, you have a battle in your hands. A battle between the powers that be and the powers that should be. You and I are the latter. With the power drawn from your naga bloodline and the power drawn from my witch bloodline, we make a potent combination."

Wiping her eyes, Anitha asked feebly, "To do what?"

"Destroy the current corrupt order and replace it with a new Sacred Earth based on compassion and symbiosis. The apocalypse in your dreams need not happen, not if we intercede."

"You're crazy." Anitha sighed. "I screwed up my dreamtime. My power is unreliable."

"You will learn in time to manage your power. Don't worry. Besides, what do we have to lose?"

Anitha reminded herself of Kamini Smith in a coma and her young children waiting for their mother to wake up. What if she did not? Anitha shivered as a sudden cold air wrapped itself around her. "Our humanity?"

Tilly scoffed. "Humanity is lost on humans. They

are irredeemable. It is now up to those like us, our kinds, the original, divinely approved stewards of the earth, to restore the glory of Mother Earth."

A fiery gold shone in Anitha's eyes. Her naga blood buzzed and crackled. Heat and ice coursed through her limbs. Suddenly, she felt awakened. "I see you," she said to Tilly.

Tilly leaned in to hug Anitha, whispering in a silky tone, "I see you too." Her blue pupils melted into pools of pearly moons. "From the moment I noticed you in the college bus, I saw it – you and me – I saw you and me – The Future of the Earth."

A stillness descended. The guest room was filled with the steady breaths of the girls. A sliver of smile toyed on Tilly's lips. "Well?"

"I see it too," Anitha answered.

CHAPTER TWENTY-SIX

2nd Week of January

Anitha closed the curtain for the night and finished the last of her warm oat milk, infused with turmeric and sweetened with maple syrup. It was her favourite bedtime brew. Today had been a good day. It was a relief to be back in college. Classes were exciting and the teachers were certainly welcoming. Despite the winter frost, she and Tilly went to see the horses on the field during the lunch hour and ate their sandwiches. There were other students and teachers there as well, enjoying the chilly, fresh outdoors.

Yawning, Anitha slipped under her duvet and curled snugly for the night.

Suddenly, she shivered. It was cold. Really cold in the

bedroom. Opening her sleepy eyes, she noticed that the window was open. The wintry air was blowing in. She heard the sound of the river flowing. Puzzled, she dragged herself out of bed and went to the window. The Ouse was a long stretch of meandering darkness. Ripples bobbed gently as it reflected the gleaming pearl of the full moon. Anitha looked up.

Looming eerily close above her was the moon, the white-watcher of the night sky, as though watching, waiting, observing. A ring of stars, equally white, unblinking and each one equidistant from the next one, encircled the moon in wreath-like fashion. Transfixed, Anitha held her breath.

And then, it happened. Like a wheel, the stars rotated on their fixed points. Anitha blinked. She was scared. The moon began to ease into a gradual spin. Anitha screamed for her mother but the words came out silent. Sparks pulsed. The moon spun at an ever-increasing pace, inching closer and closer and faster and faster towards her bedroom window. Suddenly, the moon and stars were right in front of her. Anitha juddered as waves of magnetic pulses pulled her towards the spinning disc of the moon which was now a thrumming blur of white.

Vortex 1

The giant snake stood waiting on the other side as Anitha struggled to balance herself on her feet. Scales of bluish green glittered before her. "Sol?" He did not reply. "What are you doing? Is this a dream? Are you in my head again?" The space around her was a foggy white.

"Kamini Smith is in a coma. She could die. You injected more venom than required." Solomon hissed.

"I did. She deserves it. She is a corporate psychopath."

"You have turned rogue."

"What are you now? My moral police? I want to go back to my room."

"You don't get to choose, Ani, who gets to die and who does not. Remember last year, at the slipway? You removed the poisons from your cousins because you said it was the right thing to do. It was not about your personal judgement."

"Kamini represents all that is reprehensible in the face of climate crisis." Anitha craned her neck upwards to face Solomon. He was making her angry with his holier-than-thou attitude. "Mother Earth is dying because of people like her. I can't just sit back and not do anything."

"You can do something but not this way, Ani. Please. An eye for an eye does not help with the evolution of this planet. You and I are meant to do things differently with our powers."

Anitha's skin tingled, slipping and sliding across her limbs. Her human skin merged and mingled with her naga scales. She was changing. Within seconds, she too was all glinting scales and flicked her forked tongue at Solomon. Strands of her long, black hair twisted and writhed, hissing and spitting venom. "How dare you interrupt my sleep!" Swiftly, she leapt high upon his massive shoulders and was about to spit poison into his eyes when Solomon with his gigantic right hand, swatted her away like the fly she was to him. With a thud, she landed on the ground, dizzy with disorientation. "You hit me!" she burst, helplessly.

"Anitha!" Solomon helped her up. "I am sorry."

"Get away from me!" Anitha shouted, her slithering strands of hair now resembling coils of live wire. She spotted the spinning disc of moon and stars. It was her way out...or in – back into her bedroom. Mustering all her strength, she dashed towards the moon and stars and leapt into the vortex.

Vortex 2

Exhausted, she took a moment to catch her breath. Her head throbbed and it was as if her eyes were covered in gauzy film. She rubbed them and blinked a few times before searching around. This was not her bedroom. Once more, she was surrounded by white fog. She swore. Fear pounded with the beat of her heart. She needed to jump into the vortex again.

A hissing rumble set her heart sinking. Solomon was

coming through the spinning moon and stars – his sun-gold and sea-blue scales all merged into one slithering giant serpent. Pretending to be unafraid, Anitha forced herself to pose militantly in front of the 9 foot creature as he landed gracefully on his webbed feet.

"Coward!" Anitha spat. "Pick on someone your own size!"

Calmly, Solomon hissed. His scales were now churning a hypnotic swirl of turquoise gold – a serpentine tango of water and fire. Anitha felt his heat searing into her scales but within, she shivered as spears of ice coursed through her veins. Behind Sol, the moon and stars spun. She needed to get through the vortex. To get back home. To her bed. To her own sleep. Back to the dream of her own making. Not Sol's. She made a run for it.

Solomon roared as he swept her into his arms and pinned her to the ground. "Anitha." His voice was low and kind. He was on top of her, his scaly face too close to her own.

"What are you doing?" Anitha stammered. She could not move beneath his weight.

Without a word, Solomon hissed. Flicking his tongue, he touched the tip of her quivering nose and pressed his lips upon hers, spewing venomous fire and water into her mouth.

Her throat burned.

Her limbs froze.
She was burning and freezing.
Burning.
Freezing.
"I'm dying," Anitha thought. "I'm dying."

Dream within a Dream

Chemical smells filled the air. The walls and floors were white. A girl and a boy were crying. They were very young. A woman laid on the bed, propped by machines and gadgets. Kamini Smith. Their mother. There was a man too, thin with red, swollen eyes. The air was thick with unbelievable pain. Their pain. Anitha wanted to disappear. She did not want to feel their pain but their emotions slipped through her anyway.

Their tears became her tears. Their grief, her grief and their loss, her loss. When they wailed, she wailed. There was no difference between her and them. They merged into her and she merged into them in one single breath. Anitha coughed and choked and gasped for air.

Emptiness swallowed her.
Peace.
Quiet.

Her eyes opened. She was still in the hospital. Suffering filled the air. Filled her. Kamini was still in a coma. And

Anitha knew. She understood. It was time to do the right thing.

She slithered towards Kamini.

CHAPTER TWENTY-SEVEN

Days Later

"Lunch will be ready in a couple of hours," reminded Durga as Anitha and Solomon prepared to go for a walk in the woods.

"Yes, Ma." Anitha slipped on her gloves.

"You sure you're up to it? I mean..." Durga eyed Solomon. "It's been less than a week since your dreamtime."

"The walk will do me good."

Solomon assured, "She's with me. She'll be fine, I promise."

The sun was bright, melting the overnight frost. The pair walked for a while, simply listening to the sounds of people and wildlife around them. Anitha considered the events of the past few months. She admitted her body was weak, but her mind was strong and lucid. She had learned so much from her dreamtimes and decided to take Tilly's advice and start on her own Book of Naga during the spring holidays. She looked forward to dedicating her time to this.

From the hedges, a cat appeared, meowing. "YinYang!" Anitha knelt to stroke him. He purred.

Solomon said, "Looks like Ally has done him good. He looks well."

"I'm sure Ally would say he has done her good." YinYang purred once more before going his own way. The teenagers walked till they reached The Greenway and went in the direction of the wood.

"Sorry about the dreamtime, Ani. It must have been a shock but I did not know what else to do," Solomon apologised.

Anitha bit her lip. "Well, don't get into my head again. It's weird. I mean it."

"At least in your head I kissed you."

Anitha punched Solomon lightly on his arm. "That was not exactly my idea of a kiss."

"Close enough," defended Solomon. "It will do. For now."

They entered the wood. It was darker and quieter.

Anitha went towards the river. She remembered the cobra shaped wave, swallowing Solomon and her into its grip during the first dreamtime. Her grandmother.

"Hey, Sol, thanks for making me do the right thing."

"You did it. You entered into a state of understanding of your own freewill. Kamini will fully recover in a few months. What she does after that is up to her. She has been given the vision."

"We live and learn, huh?"

"Shhh –" Solomon motioned to Anitha to stop talking. "See." He pointed to a long, slim, furry body from behind a yew. The russet-hued creature was intently watching them.

"A fox!" whispered Anitha, excitedly. "I have an apple in my pocket. Half-eaten."

"He will love that. Go on."

The fox eyed her, timid but tempted. He edged nearer but quickly retreated. Anitha placed the apple on the ground. She and Solomon stepped back. The fox came forward, gripped the apple in his mouth and stared at them before trotting off into the inner sanctum of the wood.

"Now that was special!" exclaimed Anitha, her eyes, laughing.

Solomon turned to his friend. He had not seen her

this happy for a long time. The dappled afternoon sun sparkled in her warm, dark eyes. He touched the small of her back lightly. "Hey, you…"

"Yes?"

"We can still do this you know, you and me…help save Mother Earth."

Anitha smiled. Her eyes were still laughing. "I know," she said, "I know."

The next morning, Anitha woke up, inspired to compose this poem and include it in her Book of Naga.

The Seeing

I rise and shine
from my serpent shrine
and slither my way
through the day.
My call shines bright before me...
Now I see
Now I see
as I rise and shine
from my serpent shrine

H

    I

        S

           S

ACKNOWLEDGEMENTS

For Olivia, Caroline, Melissa, Nina & Karen for the artful and loving midwifery skills in birthing this second book. Forever thanks.

Find us online

at

ragged-bears.com

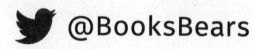 @BooksBears

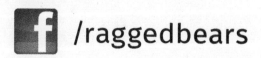 /raggedbears

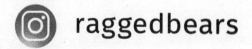 raggedbears